Cupid The Dog And Valentine's Day.

By Jane J. Miller.

a brighter and happier place.
Nic

Copyright ©2022 By Jane J. Miller.

Once upon a time, a sweet and playful puppy named Cupid lived in a cozy little house on the edge of a bustling city.

Cupid was a fluffy little ball of energy with soft white and brown fur and a wagging tail that never seemed to stop.

Cupid loved nothing more than running around the house and yard, chasing after toys, and playing with his human family.

But there was one day of the year that Cupid looked forward to more than any other - Valentine's Day.

On Valentine's Day, Cupid's family would always do something special to celebrate the holiday of love.

They would decorate the house with red and pink streamers, bake heart-shaped cookies, and exchange sweet cards and gifts with each other.

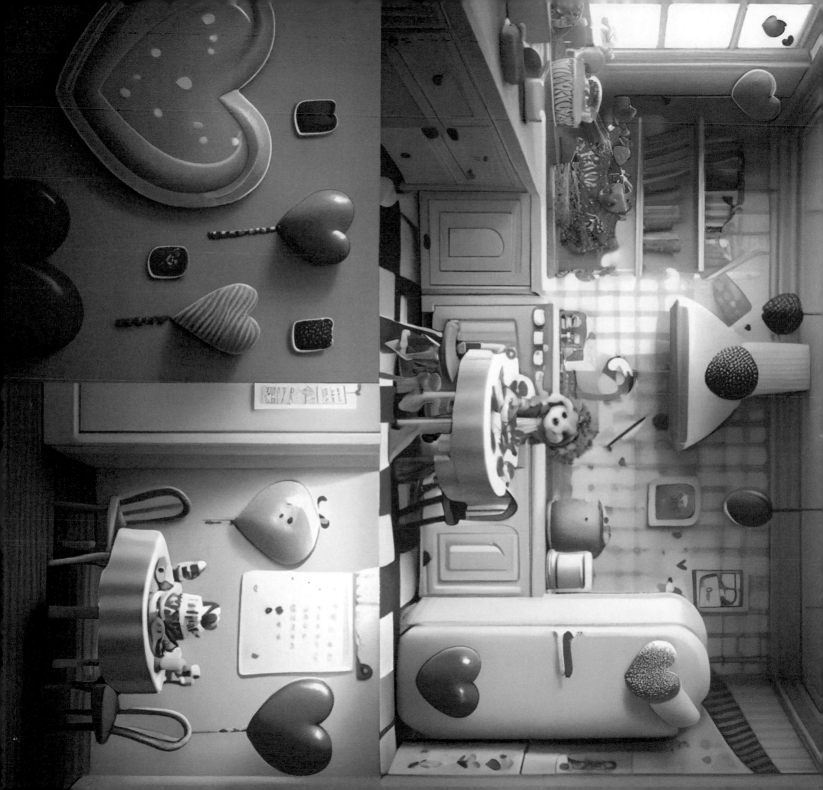

Cupid loved being a part of the celebration, and he always tried to help out however he could. He would bark excitedly as his family hung up the decorations and eagerly begged for a taste of the cookies as they came out of the oven.

But most of all,
Cupid loved to be the center
of attention on Valentine's Day.
He would wag his tail and
do all sorts of tricks to make
his family laugh and show them
how much he loved them.

One year, as Cupid was running around the house, he suddenly had a brilliant idea. He would use his special powers as a puppy to help spread love and happiness to all the people in the world.

Cupid ran to his family and told them about his plan. They were slightly surprised, but they knew Cupid was an exceptional puppy with a big heart. So they decided to help him out.

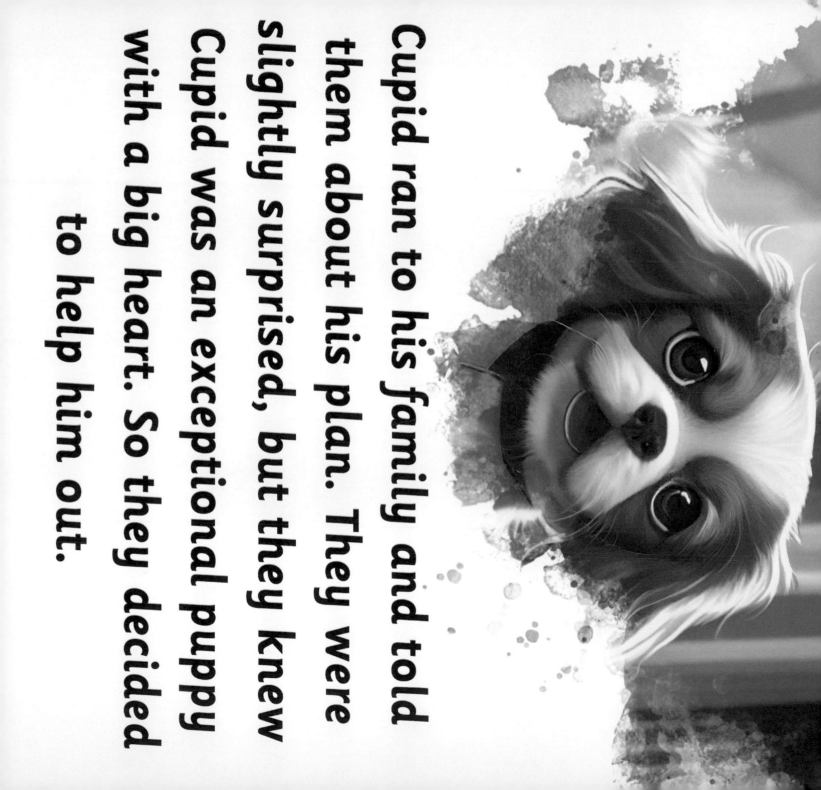

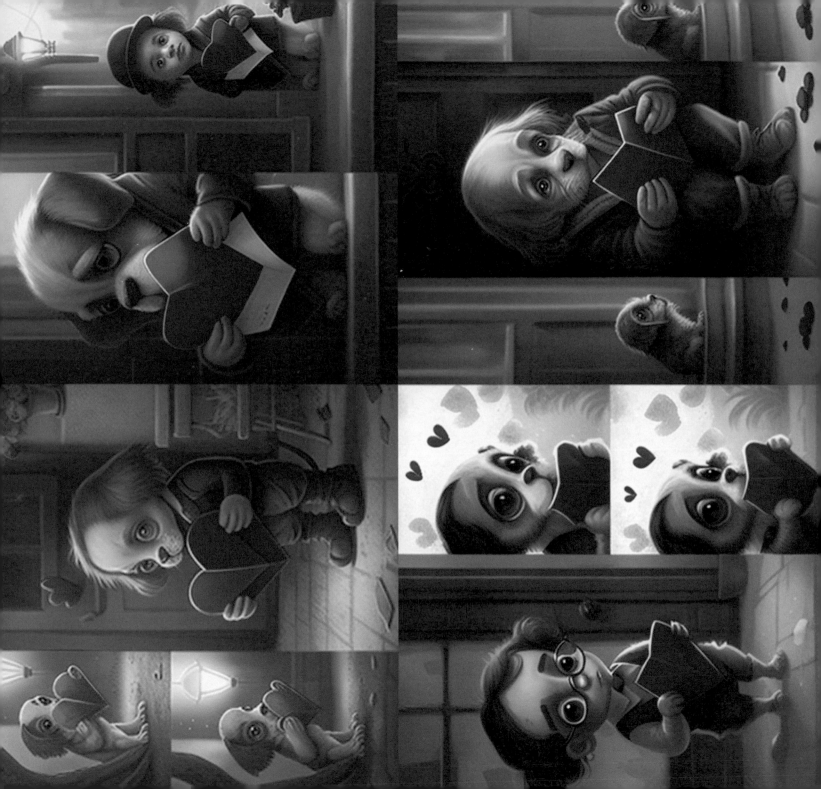

Cupid and his family set out on
a mission to spread love and
happiness to everyone they met.
They went from door to door,
delivering handmade cards
and little gifts to all their friends
and neighbors.

As they walked through the streets, Cupid's tail wagged with excitement.

He had never felt so happy and full of love before.

And as they went from house to house, he could see their small acts of kindness brought joy and happiness to the people they met.

In the end, Cupid's mission was a great success. People were smiling and laughing everywhere he went, spreading love and happiness to each other. And Cupid knew he he had played a small part in making the world brighter and happier.

Cupid and his family returned home, tired but happy as the day ended. They sat in the cozy living room and exchanged Valentine's Day cards and gifts with each other, surrounded by the warmth and love of their memorable holiday.

Cupid knew he would always
treasure these special memories
of the love and happiness
he had helped spread.

The End.

Thank you for purchasing our book! We hope you enjoyed reading it as much as we enjoyed creating it.

We value your feedback and would be grateful if you could take a few moments to leave a review on Amazon. Your review helps other readers discover our books and helps us improve as authors.

Thank you for your support. ♡ ♡ ♡

Sincerely,

Jane J. Miller.

Printed in Great Britain
by Amazon

18152689R00022